Cloudette

tom lichtenheld

Christy Ottaviano Books
HENRY HOLT AND COMPANY • NEW YORK

To all the kids at the schools I've visited:
This book was inspired by your energy and imagination.

Special thanks to Christy Ottaviano, Christina Calvit,
Amy Krouse Rosenthal, and Jessica Miller

With love and gratitude to Jan

Henry Holt and Company, LLC
Publishers since 1866
175 Fifth Avenue
New York, New York 10010
www.HenryHoltKids.com

Distributed in Canada by H. B. Fenn and Company Ltd.

Library of Congress Cataloging-in-Publication Data
Lichtenheld, Tom.
Cloudette / by Tom Lichtenheld. — 1st ed.
p. cm.
"Christy Ottaviano Books."
Summary: Cloudette, the littlest cloud, finds a way to do something big and important like the other clouds do.
ISBN 978-0-8050-8776-5
[1. Clouds—Fiction. 2. Size—Fiction. 3. Rain and rainfall—Fiction.] I. Title.
PZ7.L592Clo 2011 [E]—dc22 2010011688

First Edition—2011

The illustrations are rendered in ink, pastel, colored pencil, and watercolor. The water part of the watercolor was collected in a bucket during a rainstorm, so this book is partially made of clouds. Thank you, clouds.

Printed in December 2010 in China by Macmillan Production (Asia) Ltd., Kwun Tong, Kowloon, Hong Kong (Supplier Code 10), on acid-free paper. ∞

In case you want to use this book as a rocket:

10 9 8 7 6 5 4 3 2 1 blastoff!

Cloudette was a cloud.
A very small cloud.

Usually, Cloudette didn't mind being smaller than the average cloud.

In fact, being small
had lots of advantages.

Everyone called her cute little names.

She had lots of little friends.

No matter how crowded it was,
she could always find a good spot
to watch fireworks.

She could sneak through tight spaces,

hide in small places,

and she even had a special
little space that always made
her feel cozy at night.

But once in a while, all the other clouds would run off to do something big and important.

And make some mighty rivers flow.
No, thanks. I'll just watch from here.

Cloudette could see them in the distance, doing
all sorts of important cloud things.

This made her want to do big and important things, too.

She wanted to make a garden grow.

She wanted
to make
a brook
babble.

She

wanted

to

make

a

waterfall

fall.

And she thought nothing would be more fun than giving some kids a day off from school.

One night, Cloudette lay awake wondering
what she could do that was big and important.

She thought maybe she could work for the fire department.

Or maybe they needed some help down at the garden center.

But nobody seemed to need her.

Cloudette was feeling blue.

The next day, there was a big storm in Cloudette's neighborhood.

The sky got dark, the rain came down like cats and dogs, and the wind blew harder than she'd ever seen wind blow before.

When the storm finally stopped,
Cloudette realized she'd been blown
far from her neighborhood.

She didn't know anyone here.

And they didn't seem eager to get to know her.

But pretty soon she was making new friends and seeing things she'd never seen before.

Then she heard something she'd never heard before.

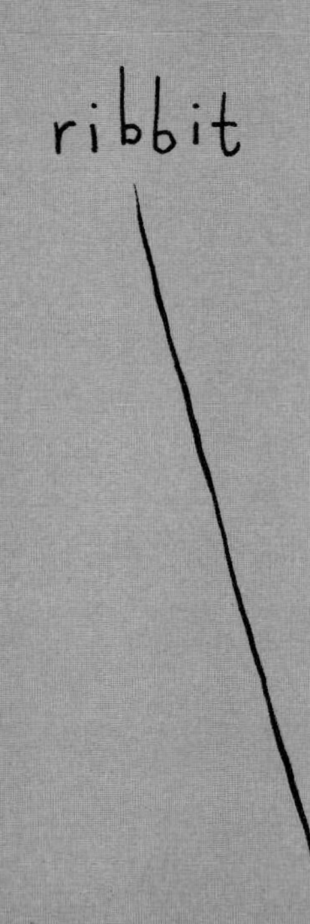

She looked down at what was supposed to be a pond,
but was really just a puddle of mud.

This gave Cloudette an idea . . .

More like a brainstorm, actually.

She held
her breath until
she started to
puff up all over.

Then she turned a
nice blue-gray color.

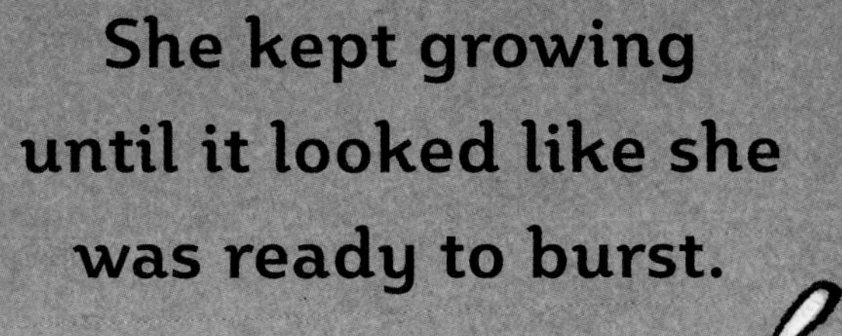

She kept growing
until it looked like she
was ready to burst.

She shook her behind
until it made a little
rumbling sound—not quite
what you'd call thunder,
but enough to let people
know they might want to
grab an umbrella.

Then she did what she'd
wanted to do for ages.

She

let

it

pour.

Cloudette rained on
that little puddle until it
grew into a big puddle.

And she kept on raining
until that big puddle

grew into a perfect pond.

As soon as she stopped, frogs of every stripe
(and spot) came jumping into the pond.

They all let out a big "Thank you!" in unison.

Cloudette was
exhausted, but happy.

*"Thank you!" in Frog

Nice work, cloudy.
Yeah, way to water!
Prodigious precipitation, pipsqueak!
Even the higher-ups were impressed, which got her thinking . . .

That was some righteous rain!
We knew you had it in you!

I'll bet there are other
big and important things
a little cloud can do.

And off she went.

the end